A HILDA BOSWELL Little Treasury

Stories · Poems · Rhymes

COLLINS COLOUR CUBS

GREEN Treasury

A HILDA BOSWELL Little Treasury

Stories · Poems · Rhymes

COLLINS COLOUR CUBS

GREEN
Treasury

Goldilocks and The Three Bears

There was once a little girl called Goldilocks who lived with her mother and father in a house near a wood. One bright summer morning, Goldilocks went into the wood to gather wild flowers. She had often been told not to wander too far away, but this morning she forgot. There always seemed to be lovelier flowers a little farther on. Presently she came to a cottage in a clearing.

"I wonder who lives there?" she said.

She was a very bold little girl. She walked straight up and knocked on the door. There was no answer, so she lifted the latch and walked in.

She was in the living-room, and on the table stood three bowls of porridge. A big bowl, a middle-size bowl, and a little bowl. The smell of the porridge made her feel hungry so she tasted a spoonful from the big bowl, but it was too hot. She tasted a spoonful from the middle-size bowl, but it was too cold. Then she tasted a spoonful from the little bowl and it was just right, so she ate up all the porridge.

Then she noticed three chairs. A big chair, a middle-size chair, and a little chair.

Goldilocks sat down on the big chair, but it was too hard. She sat down on the middle-size chair, but it was too soft. Then she sat down on the little chair and it felt just right, until *bang!* the bottom fell out!

Upstairs in the bedroom, Goldilocks saw three beds. A big bed, a middle-size bed, and a little bed. Suddenly she felt very sleepy and lay down on the big bed, but it was too hard. The middle-size bed was too soft, but the little bed was just right, and in no time at all Goldilocks was fast asleep.

Now, the cottage belonged to a family of bears who had gone out for a walk while their porridge cooled. When they got back, they knew that someone had been in the house.

"Who's been tasting *my* porridge?" growled Father Bear. "And *my* porridge?" cried Mother Bear. "*My* porridge is all eaten up!" squeaked Baby Bear.

Then the bears looked at their chairs.

"Who's been sitting in *my* chair?" growled Father Bear. "Who's been sitting in *my* chair?" cried Mother Bear.

"And who's been sitting in *my* chair and broken it!" squeaked Baby Bear.

Now the bears were very cross and went upstairs to look in their bedroom.

"Who's been lying on *my* bed?" growled Father Bear.

"And who's been lying on *my* bed?" cried Mother Bear.

"And look who's lying on *my* bed," squeaked Baby Bear. "It's a little girl!"

There lay Goldilocks, her head on Baby Bear's pillow.

"Well!" growled Father Bear. "Well!" cried Mother Bear. "Well!" squeaked Baby Bear.

The sound of their voices, all growling and crying and squeaking together, was so strange and so loud that Goldilocks heard it, even in her sleep, and she woke in a fright. She sat up in the little bear's bed and screamed at the sight of the three furry faces gazing at her.

"Poor thing!" said Mother Bear, patting her head gently with her big paw.

Goldilocks and the three bears went downstairs and out of the cottage. Father Bear showed her the way out of the wood and Mother Bear and Baby Bear waved goodbye until she was out of sight.

And Goldilocks never saw them again.

HUSH A BYE BABY

Hush-a-bye, baby,
  on the tree-top,
When the wind blows
  the cradle will rock;
When the bough breaks
  the cradle will fall,
And down will come baby,
  cradle and all.

The Jumblies

They went to sea in a Sieve, they did,
  In a Sieve they went to sea;
In spite of all their friends could say,
  On a winter's morn, on a stormy day,
In a Sieve they went to sea!

And when the Sieve turned round and round,
  And everyone cried: 'You'll all be
                              drowned!'
They cried aloud: 'Our Sieve ain't big,
  But we don't care a button, we don't
                              care a fig!
In a Sieve we'll go to sea!'

Far and few, far and few,
  Are the lands where the Jumblies live;
Their heads are green and their hands
                              are blue,
  And they went to sea in a Sieve.

EDWARD LEAR

Diddle, Diddle, Dumpling

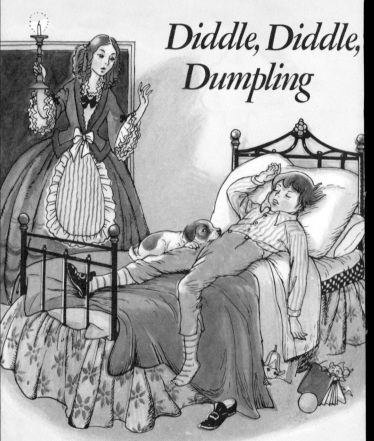

Diddle, diddle, dumpling, my son John,
Went to bed with his trousers on;
One shoe off, and one shoe on,
Diddle, diddle, dumpling, my son John.

DOCTOR FOSTER

Doctor Foster went to Gloucester
In a shower of rain;
He stepped in a puddle,
Right up to his middle,
And never went there again.

Grasshopper Green

Grasshopper Green is a comical
chap;
He lives on the best of fare.
Bright little trousers, jacket
and cap,
These are his summer wear.

Out in the meadow he loves to go,
Playing away in the sun;
It's hopperty, skipperty,
high and low,
Summer's the time for fun.

Grasshopper Green has a quaint
little house;
It's under the hedge so gay.
Grandmother Spider, as still as
a mouse,
Watches him over the way.

Gladly he's calling the children,
I know,
Out in the beautiful sun;
It's hopperty, skipperty,
high and low,
Summer's the time for fun.

Georgie Porgie

Georgie Porgie, pudding and pie,
 Kissed the girls and made them cry.
When the boys came out to play,
 Georgie Porgie ran away.

CURLY LOCKS

Curly Locks! Curly Locks!
  Will you be mine?
You shall not wash dishes,
  Nor yet feed the swine;
But sit on a cushion,
  And sew a fine seam,
And feed upon strawberries,
  Sugar
      and
          cream.

The Winds
They Did Blow

The winds they did blow;
  The leaves they did wag;
Along came a beggar boy,
  And put me in his bag.

He took me up to London;
  A lady me did buy,
She put me in a silver cage,
  And hung me up on high.

With apples by the fire,
  And nuts for to crack,
Besides a little feather bed
  To rest my little back.

Time to Rise

A birdie with a yellow bill
Hopped upon the window-sill,
Cocked his shining eye and said:
'Ain't you 'shamed, you sleepy-head?'

ROBERT LOUIS STEVENSON

Little Girl, Little Girl

Little girl, little girl,
   Where have you been?
Gathering roses
   To give to the Queen.

Little girl, little girl,
   What gave she you?
She gave me a diamond
   As big as my shoe.

A ROBIN AND A ROBIN'S SON

A robin and a robin's son,
  Once went to town to buy a bun,
They couldn't decide on plum or plain,
  And so they went back home again.

The Pied Piper

This is the strange story of what happened a long time ago in the old German town of Hamelin.

Hamelin was as pleasant a town as you could ever wish to live in. The houses, with their crooked gables, leaned towards each other across the street. The church spires rose high above the tiled roofs, and outside the town wall flowed the broad and shining River Weser.

Now whether it was because the harvest that year had been an especially good one with plenty of grain in the barns, or whether it was because of the carelessness of the good people of Hamelin who had enough food and to spare in their larders, I do not know . . . .

But one terrible year, the town found that it had been invaded by an army of rats. Life became a great misery for the people of Hamelin for the rats were everywhere, spoiling the food and terrifying the children. Rats in their beds and in their boots, in the cupboards and on the shelves, gnawing and scratching and squeaking. Brown rats, grey rats, black rats. Rats with fierce whiskers and rats with long tails. Young rats and old rats.

They scratched behind the walls, scurried about the kitchens, ran in and out of the houses, hundreds and thousands of them, all squeaking at the tops of their voices.

They killed the cats and fought the dogs. The people set traps but the rats were too clever to get caught.

The Hamelin people grew so worried that they flocked to the town hall and told the mayor that he must *do* something.

The mayor and the aldermen had been sitting around the council table day after day, worrying and arguing about nothing else but RATS! But what *could* they do? The mayor scratched his head and the treasurer did some sums and the secretary wrote it all down, but still they didn't know how to get rid of the rats. As they sat fretting, there came a light rap on the door, then the door opened gently and a very strange figure entered.

The strangest thing about him was his long coat of different colours. The mayor thought he must be a strolling minstrel for he carried a musical pipe, holding it lovingly as though he longed to play.

He was tall and lean, and his appearance frightened the aldermen a little, but his smile was kind and his sharp eyes twinkled merrily as he walked up to the table.

"Please, your honours," he said softly, "I know a charm that will rid you of the rats."

"Who are you?" gasped the mayor.

"They call me the Pied Piper," he replied, and indeed, the name suited him. As he spoke, his fingers tapped on the pipe as if they itched to play. "My price is a thousand guilders," said the piper.

"Fifty thousand!" shouted the mayor. "No price is too high for a service like that!" He smiled at the treasurer and the treasurer nodded, and all the aldermen nodded.

"I ask for one thousand," murmured the Pied Piper. "A bargain is a bargain."

The Pied Piper stepped out into the street and raised the magic pipe to his lips. At the sound of the first note there was a pitter-patter on the cobblestones as out of the houses came the rats. The piper played a strange, eerie tune and the great army of rats followed him.

The noise of the scampering rats grew louder and louder, swelling to a tremendous roar as the thousands of rats tumbled out from every nook and cranny of the old town.

The mayor and aldermen watched from the steps of the town hall and the people stared from their doorways as the piper led the rats out of the town. Right to the banks of the river he led them, and the creatures were so bewitched by the wild music they plunged into the fast-flowing River Weser.

The people of
Hamelin gave a great
cheer to be rid of
the rats. Every bell
in every steeple rang
and the children
danced in the
streets. The mayor's
face beamed with
pleasure – until he
saw the tall figure of
the Pied Piper and
remembered his
bargain. He frowned.
Fifty thousand
guilders!

"My thousand guilders, please," said the Pied Piper.

"A thousand guilders to a wandering gypsy!" thought the mayor. "The rats are all drowned. He can't bring them back!"

"A thousand guilders!" he said to the piper. "Come now, my good fellow, that was only a joke. I will give you fifty."

The gentle smile on the piper's face changed to a frown. "If you cheat me," he said, "I shall play a different tune. One you won't like."

"You can play till you burst, for all I care!" said the mayor angrily, and paid him nothing.

The mayor and the people of Hamelin cared nothing for the Pied Piper now that they were rid of the rats.

Now that their worries were over, they were ready to make fun of the comical stranger. They laughed and pointed at him as he walked calmly out of the market-place.

The piper said nothing, but he lifted the pipe to his lips and started to play. It was a tune full of enchantment, the notes sweet and clear as a birdcall. To the horror of every grown-up person in Hamelin, the children started to stream out of the houses and follow the Pied Piper, leaping and laughing happily and clapping their hands. Tumbling and skipping and never taking their eyes from him, they followed the Pied Piper through the streets of Hamelin and out of the town towards the mountains. The sweet, enchanted music was for them alone and they could hear nothing else.

"Come back! Oh, please come back!" pleaded their mothers.

But they could not turn back. They were under a spell of enchantment that nothing could break. With hearts as heavy as stones, the parents watched as their children danced joyfully away.

They followed the piper through fields and over streams until they reached a mountain that rose high above the town. He led them to the opening of a cave and without a backward glance, all the children streamed in and the cave closed behind them for ever.

Well, not *all*. One little lame boy had not been able to keep up with his friends and was left behind. He turned sadly back to Hamelin where his parents wept for joy to see him, but he wept from sorrow.

He told them that the sweet notes of the magic pipe had told him about a wonderful country, more wonderful and beautiful than anyone could ever dream, where there was nothing but happiness, and where no one was ever sad or lame or tired.

As the years went by, other children were born in Hamelin, but no one could ever forget the story of the Pied Piper, and for one of the Hamelin churches, an artist made a window in coloured glass, showing the procession of little children following the tall figure of the Pied Piper.

The Was an Old Man on the Border

There was an old man on the Border,
Who lived in the utmost disorder;
    He danced with the cat,
    And made tea in his hat,
Which vexed all the folks on the Border.

There Was an Old Man with a Beard

There was an old man with a beard,
Who said: 'It is just as I feared!
    Two Owls and a Hen,
    Four Larks and a Wren,
Have all built their nests in my beard!'

Wee Little House with the Golden Thatch

Wee little house with the golden thatch
Twice I knocked and I lifted the latch
'And pray, is the mistress here?'
'In black stuff gown and yellow vest,
She's busily packing her honey-chest;
Will you taste a bit, my dear?'

THE LITTLE LAND

When at home alone I sit
And am very tired of it,
I have just to shut my eyes
To go sailing through the
                                        skies –

To go sailing far away
To the pleasant Land of Play;
To the fairy land afar
Where the Little People are.

ROBERT LOUIS STEVENSON

Come Let's to Bed

'Come let's to bed,' says Sleepy Head,
'Tarry awhile,' says Slow.
'Put on the pan,' says Greedy Nan,
'We'll sup before we go.'

Pussy-cat Pussy-cat

Pussy-cat, pussy-cat,
Where have you been?

I've been to London
To look at the Queen.

Pussy-cat, pussy-cat,
What did you there?

I frightened a little mouse
Under her chair.

TOM TOM THE PIPER'S SON

Tom, Tom, the Piper's son,
  Stole a pig and away he run.
The pig was eat,
And Tom was beat,
  And Tom went roaring down the street.

Here A Little Child I Stand

Here a little child I stand,
Heaving up my either hand;
Cold as paddocks though they be;
Here I lift them up to Thee,
For a benison to fall
On our meat and on us all.

ROBERT HERRICK

Ladybird, Ladybird

Ladybird, Ladybird,
  Fly away home,
Your house is on fire
  And your children all gone;
All except one,
  And that's little Ann,
And she has crept under
  The dripping pan.

THE BABES IN THE WOOD

Once upon a time, two children lived in a big house on the borders of a wood. Their parents, who loved them very dearly, were rich enough to buy them everything they wished for, and all day long they played in the beautiful garden.

But one sad day, their father and mother died and the sister and brother were left alone.

The children had an uncle whom they had never seen. He lived far away across the seas; but as soon as he learned of the death of his brother, the children's father, he hurried to their home. He knew that now their father was dead, the children would have all his money, and the uncle also knew that if he could get rid of the children all this money would be his.

The more he thought about this money the more he longed for it. And then a dreadful thought came into his head.

He would kill the children and take the money. So he hired two robbers, and paid them to take the children to a lonely spot in the wood and kill them.

One morning, the robbers crept into the garden where the children were playing and took them away. The men led them out into the wood, and on and on till they came to a deserted spot. They had come a long way and the children were glad to rest. They sat down on the trunk of a tree while the robbers moved away and spoke in low voices.

"Why kill them?" said one. "Let's leave them, and perhaps someone may find them and give them shelter."

The little girl crept closer to her brother. Then the other robber came and spoke to them.

"Stay here while we go to find food and shelter for the night," he said gruffly.

But it was a lie.

They went away,
and the children
were left all alone in
the wood. They had
come too far to be
able to find the way
back and so they
wandered on, hoping
to find shelter. For a
time they were
happy walking
among the ferns and
wild flowers, but
soon the sun went
down and a great
stillness came over
the wood. At last
the children sat
down under an oak
tree and fell asleep.

The shy squirrels with their long bushy tails glanced wonderingly at them. And the gentle wind shook the leaves so that they fell, making a cloak to cover them.

When morning came, all the creatures rushed about finding food for the children. The squirrels brought nuts, the birds brought berries, and Robin told them which ones would be safe for children to eat. Even the owl went back to his house in the tree and brought them each a tasty morsel. Old Grandpa Fieldmouse wasn't best pleased.

Then Robin said: "I shall fly off and find someone who will take care of them."

"How can you tell them that the children are here?" asked the wise owl.

"Leave that to me," said Robin and he flew down and tweaked a button from the little boy's coat.

Then Squirrel frisked down the tree.

He nibbled the little girl's hair-ribbon with his sharp teeth till he had cut right through. Then he handed the tiny piece to the robin.

Soon Robin was ready to set out. The blue ribbon was tied neatly around his throat, and in his beak he carried the bright, shiny button. He flew straight to a cottage on the edge of the wood. The old woman who lived there was his friend, for she never forgot to put out crumbs for him. He perched on a branch by the cottage door and sang his loudest.

"Bless me!" said the old woman. "There's my friend, the little robin!"

Robin flew down and dropped the bright, shiny button at her feet.

"Bless me!" said the old woman when she recognised the button from her little grandson's coat. And when she glanced back at the little robin she recognised the blue ribbon from her little granddaughter's cap.

Robin flew a little way off and sang again and the old woman put on her shawl and followed him. Robin led her to the heart of the wood.

"Bless me!" cried the old woman when she saw her two little grandchildren.

"Oh, Grannie!" said the little boy. "We had such a horrid dream!"

"Bless me!" said the old woman. "That's all over now."

THE
HILDA BOSWELL
LITTLE TREASURIES
are derived from
HILDA BOSWELL'S
TREASURY OF NURSERY RHYMES
TREASURY OF FAIRY TALES
TREASURY OF POETRY
TREASURY OF CHILDREN'S STORIES
and
A CHILD'S GARDEN OF VERSES by
Robert Louis Stevenson

ISBN 0 00 123583 4
Copyright © 1980 Wm. Collins Sons & Co. Ltd.
Printed in Great Britain

HOPPER
COT